10 Minute Tales

Fireman Sam

The Pontypandy Pioneers

When you see these symbols:

Read aloud
Read aloud to your child.

Read alone
Support your child as they read alone.

Read along
Read along with your child.

EGMONT
We bring stories to life

FSC
www.fsc.org
MIX
Paper from responsible sources
FSC® C018306

Egmont is passionate about helping to preserve the world's remaining ancient forests. We only use paper from legal and sustainable forest sources.

This book is made from paper certified by the Forest Stewardship Council® (FSC®), an organisation dedicated to promoting responsible management of forest resources. For more information on the FSC®, please visit www.fsc.org. To learn more about Egmont's sustainable paper policy, please visit www.egmont.co.uk/ethical

D0102014

Read aloud   Read along

The children of Pontypandy were very excited. Fireman Sam was taking them out for a day of action and adventure!

"This day out is going to be really cool," said James. "I love being a Pontypandy Pioneer. We're the best adventure group in the world!"

"And Fireman Sam is the best leader in the world!" added Sarah.

The Pontypandy Pioneers are very excited.
They are going on an adventure with Sam.

"**I** hope we get to do rock-climbing and all sorts of scary stuff!" said Mandy, jumping up and down.

Norman was thinking of his tummy. "I hope there's plenty to eat!" he said. Just then, Norman's mum Dilys came along with a big brown bag full of food.

"Don't worry," she said. "I've packed you all a feast for lunchtime."

Soon, Sam came out of the Fire Station. "Are we all ready for a day of adventure?" he called.

Read alone

Norman hopes there will be lots of food.
"Is everybody ready?" calls Sam.

Read aloud   Read along

On Pontypandy Beach, Bronwyn Jones
was looking for pretty seashells when
she came upon something very strange.

Lots of big, wooden crates had washed up
on the shore and some were still floating about
in the sea.

"All those crates could be very dangerous
to boats," she said. "Not to mention the wildlife
on the beach. I need to call Fireman Sam!"

Read alone

Bronwyn is looking for shells. She spots lots of crates on the beach and out at sea.

At the Fire Station, Station Officer
Steele sounded the alarm.

"There's an emergency at the beach," he said,
rushing out of the Station. "Sam, we're going
to need your help."

"I'm sorry, kids," Sam said, jumping into Jupiter.
"We'll have to have our adventure another day."

The Pioneers felt really sad.

Sam is called to help with the emergency.
The children are sad that Sam has to go.

Read alone

Read aloud   Read along

"**W**hat are we going to do now?" cried Mandy. "Sam said he had a big surprise waiting for us at the end of the mountain trail."

"We can still go on our adventure," said Norman. "All we need is a new leader, and *I'm* the best person for the job!"

Dilys shook her head. "No, Norman. The leader needs to be a grown-up," she said.

So Trevor said that he would lead the Pontypandy Pioneers on their adventure day.

Read alone

Norman wants to be the leader,
but Trevor takes over instead.

Read aloud Read along

Soon, Trevor and the Pioneers were marching along the mountain trail to the Mountain Rescue Station.

"Keep up, everyone!" Norman shouted.

"Not so fast, Norman," said Trevor, panting. "I need to make sure we are going in the right direction."

Trevor took out his map, but before he had a chance to look at it a big gust of wind blew it out of his hands!

"Erm … not to worry. I know where we're going!" said Trevor.

The Pioneers go on their adventure day, but Trevor loses the map!

Back at the beach, the rescue team were busy gathering up the crates.

Sam and Penny were in Neptune, making sure all the crates were collected before they became a danger to any boats.

Tom was in his helicopter overhead. "Come in, Sam," he said over the radio. "It looks like a cargo ship spilled its crates overboard a few miles out to sea."

"Thanks, Tom," replied Sam. "We'll make sure they're all collected and get them back to the ship as soon as possible. Over."

Read alone

Tom is in his helicopter. He spots the cargo
ship that dropped the crates.

The Pontypandy Pioneers were
getting very tired and hungry. They
hadn't had any lunch, and Norman wasn't
at all sure Trevor knew where he was going.

"Maybe we should stop for something to eat,"
Trevor suggested. That soon cheered everyone
up. "Now, who's got the food?"

Mandy gulped. "We thought *you* had it!"
she said.

Trevor shook his head. "Me? No.
I thought one of *you* had it!"

Norman groaned and held
his stomach. "This is the
worst adventure day
ever!" he said.

Read alone

Trevor and the Pioneers are hungry,
but they have forgotten their packed lunch!

Read aloud   Read along

Later that afternoon, Trevor had a surprise for the Pioneers. "I know I lost the map and we forgot our lunch," he began. "But you'll be pleased to know we've reached the end of the mountain trail ... ta-dah!"

Everyone gasped. Just behind Trevor was a zip wire running from the Mountain Rescue Station to the bottom of the mountain.

"Cool!" said Sarah. "I want to go first!"

Read alone

Trevor finds the way to the end of the mountain trail. There is a zip wire to play on.

Read aloud Read along

But Norman had another idea ...
"If Sam was here, *he* would go first," he said
naughtily. "Maybe *you* should go first, Trevor.
Unless you're scared ..."

Trevor looked up at the zip wire and gulped.
"No," he said. "I ... I can do it!"

Soon, Trevor was at the start of the zip wire.
He clipped on his safety harness and took a deep
breath. He counted to three and jumped off.
"Aaargh!" he cried.

Suddenly, the zip wire jammed and Trevor
was stuck in mid-air!

Read alone

Trevor zooms down the zip wire first,
but he gets stuck!

Read aloud   Read along

"Oh no!" shouted Norman. He started to feel guilty about making Trevor go first on the zip wire. "I'll run up to the Mountain Rescue Station to tell Tom."

But Tom wasn't there. He was still helping Fireman Sam at the beach.

"I'd better call for help," said Norman, picking up the Station's radio. "Hello? Hello? Fireman Sam, are you there?"

Read alone

Norman calls Fireman Sam to come and rescue Trevor.

Back at the beach, the team had
finished clearing up the wooden crates
and returned them to the cargo ship.
Suddenly, Sam heard Norman's voice on
Jupiter's radio.

"Norman? Is that you?" asked Sam, surprised.

"Yes! I'm at the Mountain Rescue Station. Trevor's
in trouble!" Norman cried.

"We're on our way!" Sam said. He put on Jupiter's
siren and raced off.

Sam and the team have finished clearing the crates. Sam goes to help Trevor!

Trevor was holding onto the zip wire as tightly as he could, but he could feel his hands slipping. "I don't think I can hold on much longer!" he wailed.

Luckily, Fireman Sam and his team were there in a flash. They grabbed a safety blanket from Jupiter and stretched it out under Trevor. He was going to have to jump!

"Right then, Trevor," Sam called. "All you need to do is let go and we'll catch you!"

Trevor can't hold on much longer, but Sam and the team get there in the nick of time.

Read alone

Read aloud   Read along

Trevor shut his eyes and counted to three.
He was very frightened, but he knew it was
the only way to get down!

He let go and fell through the air. He landed with a
big bounce on the safety blanket and everyone
cheered!

"That was cool!" said James.

Norman agreed. "Definitely!" he said. "Do you know
what? I think you're the bravest leader we've ever
had ... apart from Sam."

Read alone

Fireman Sam and the team rescue Trevor.
Norman thinks Trevor is really brave.

Read aloud   Read along

All the Pontypandy Pioneers felt very relieved that Trevor was OK, but their tummies were still rumbling! At that moment, Dilys came along with their lunch box.

"You forgot your sandwiches!" she said, a little out of breath. "Have you all had fun?"

Norman jumped up. "Trevor was really brave, Mam!" he said. "You should have seen him on the zip wire!"

"You'll have to do it again and show me!" Dilys said.

But Trevor couldn't think of anything worse! "Hmm. Maybe another day!" he replied.

Read alone

Dilys arrives. She wants to see Trevor on the zip wire. "Maybe another day!" says Trevor.